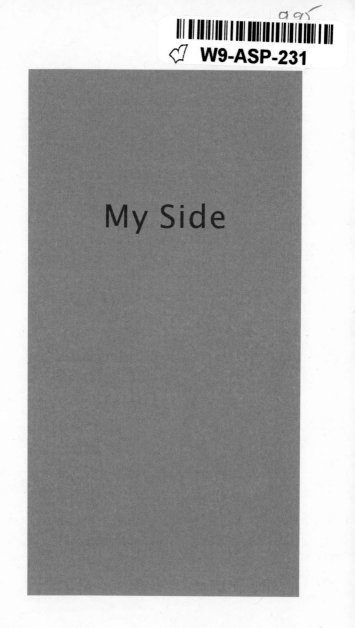

My Side

My Side

Norah McClintock

orca soundings

ORCA BOOK PUBLISHERS

Library and Archives Canada Cataloguing in Publication

McClintock, Norah
My side / Norah McClintock.
(Orca soundings)

Issued also in electronic formats.
ISBN 978-1-4598-0517-0 (bound).--ISBN 978-1-4598-0511-8 (pbk.)

I. Title. II. Series: Orca soundings
PS8575.C62M97 2013   jc813'.54   C2013-901874-3

First published in the United States, 2013

Library of Congress Control Number: 2013935297

Summary: When Addie is publicly humiliated, it is terrible,
but when she finds out her best friend was involved, it is almost unbearable.

*Orca Book Publishers is dedicated to preserving the environment and has
printed this book on Forest Stewardship Council® certified paper.*

Orca Book Publishers gratefully acknowledges the support for its publishing
programs provided by the following agencies: the Government of Canada through
the Canada Book Fund and the Canada Council for the Arts,
and the Province of British Columbia through the BC Arts Council
and the Book Publishing Tax Credit.

Cover image by Getty Images

ORCA BOOK PUBLISHERS
PO Box 5626, Stn. B
Victoria, BC Canada
V8R 6S4

ORCA BOOK PUBLISHERS
PO Box 468
Custer, WA USA
98240-0468

www.orcabook.com
Printed and bound in Canada.

16 15 14 13 • 4 3 2 1

Addie's Story

Chapter One

I stand at the curb and stare straight ahead. I am trembling all over. This is no exaggeration. My knees are shaking. My hands are shaking. My fingers are dancing, and there is nothing I can do to calm them. I am like a little kid shivering after being in the water too long, except that my lips aren't blue and my skin isn't wrinkled like a prune.

Also, I'm nowhere near the water, even though I feel as if I am drowning. I can barely breathe.

"Maybe this isn't a good idea," my dad says. He's been saying it for days.

I shake my head. "We agreed."

"I think you're underestimating—"

"I'm not." I snap the words at him like rocks launched from a slingshot. And there it is—a combination of anger, tension and terror. If I close my eyes, I am sure I will see a question flashing at me in neon letters—"Why are you doing this?"

Everyone has been saying the same thing to me—my mom, my dad, my brother by email from university, my grandma down in Phoenix, my doctor. "Addie, don't." They're like a chorus.

But if I *don't* do this, where does that leave me?

Who will I be then?

I'm late, but not *really*. It was planned this way—not by me, but by my dad—so I would get there without everyone staring at me. I went along with it, relieved.

"Maybe we should go in together," my dad says.

"We talked about this." Mostly I had done the talking. "I'm going alone."

Before my dad can say another word, I walk away from the curb, across the wide interlocking-brick patio, past the row of garbage bins and toward the entrance. My hand is still trembling when I reach out to push open the center door. My stomach heaves when I step into the empty foyer lined with glass-fronted displays of athletic trophies and team photographs. I hold my breath when I get close to the school office.

The entire outer wall of the office is glass. I could look in if I wanted to, but I tell myself I don't want to.

Still, my head turns automatically, and I spot Ms. LaPointe, one of the vice-principals, standing behind the counter. She sees me and nods. Then she turns to look at Mr. Michaud, the principal, who has just come out of his office. He follows her gaze to me. He seems surprised, even though he was told I would be here today. Maybe he thought I wouldn't show. Maybe he thought I wouldn't have the nerve. Who can blame him? I wasn't sure myself until a couple of minutes ago.

I walk up the stairs to the second floor, trying to ignore the shakiness in my knees and the churning in my stomach. The hall is deserted. Classroom doors on both sides are shut. Everyone is already inside.

I don't go to my locker. I have everything I need in my backpack. The classroom I'm headed for is at the end of the hall. As I walk toward it, the hall seems to get longer and longer, as if I'm in a nightmare and no matter how far I walk, I'll never get where I'm going.

My head spins.

I *am* in a nightmare. I've been dreading this for months. I've been praying this day would never come. But that's not the way it works. It's the day you wish for that never comes, not the one that terrifies you. *That* day rushes at you like a runaway locomotive.

Chapter Two

Mr. Grayson's head swivels around when I open the door to his classroom. My mother calls Mr. Grayson a fussy man. Mostly, the male teachers at this school dress in chinos or jeans. Mr. Grayson doesn't. He always wears a suit and tie, and nine times out of ten he has a vest on under his suit jacket.

He carries his lesson plans and test papers in a leather briefcase. No backpacks for him. He is a real stickler for propriety. And for the rules, most of which he made up and apply only to his classroom.

Rule number one is always be on time. Be in your seat on time. Hand in your assignments on time. Get your permission slips and your report cards signed on time.

Rule number two is always knock.

I don't knock, which is why his eyes are squinty behind the windows of his glasses. At first I'm sure he's going to say something sarcastic, the way he always does when someone is late or misbehaving. He does this because he knows that if there's one thing every teenager on the planet is afraid of, it's being made fun of. Being made to look and feel ridiculous. Having people laugh at him—or her.

But today he doesn't whip off a sarcastic remark. Instead, his eyes register the same surprise as Mr. Michaud's.

"Oh," he says. "It's you, Addie." He recovers enough to add, "It's good to have you back." I can't tell if he means it.

I take a seat—my seat, which is empty, as if it has been waiting for me all this time. The rasping sound as I pull out the chair fills the deep silence of the classroom.

I sit.

Mr. Grayson clears his throat and points to the board, where he has written some notes. I stare at them, but I don't copy them down. I don't volunteer any answers either. I don't even pretend to listen. It doesn't matter. Mr. Grayson goes on as if I'm not there.

I know without looking that kids are stealing glances at me. I know that one of those people is Neely. She's sitting where she has been since the beginning of the school year, over by the window. I turn and catch her sneaking a look at me. Her pale face turns crimson, and she ducks her head.

I glance at the person beside her. It's Kayla. She looks me in the eye, as if daring me to do anything to her. I meet her gaze and hold it, unblinking, until she finally looks away. When she does, I feel myself expand, as if I've devoured her. This is why I'm here. This is exactly the feeling I have been imagining.

Emboldened, I turn my attention to my next victim. John. His head is down, but I see him trying to peek at me out of the corner of his eye. It turns out he's a bigger coward than either of the girls. He doesn't look up, even though I can tell by the redness of his ears that he knows I'm watching him. He can't—or won't—acknowledge me.

Finally the bell rings. My heart begins to race. My neck tenses, then my shoulders, in what Dr. Zorbas calls preparation for fight or flight. My breath quickens. I try to slow it down by counting as I breathe—in, two, three, out, two, three. Meanwhile, all around me, kids are flooding out of the classroom. Neely almost knocks some of them over in her dash for the door. John isn't far behind her.

I take my time.

I walk slowly out of the classroom and down the hall. I know exactly where I am going to find her.

I don't want to talk to her, but I have to. At least, I think I do, right up until I catch sight of her at her locker. Her locker door is open, and she is half-hidden by it. I see flashes of her hair, not as blond now as it was two months ago. I see some girls looking at her—Shayna and Kayla and Jen. They're the girls Neely ogled all last year. They're the ones she was determined to get to know. The ones she was so desperate to hang out with. They're looking at her now, but they're not standing with her or clustered around her for support. Jen spots me and says something, her mouth half-hidden behind her hand. The other two nod. But they don't say anything to Neely. I wonder why.

I wait. Neely scurried out of class like a mouse desperate to get to its hole before the cat could trap her. She's doing her best to make herself invisible. Does she know I'm standing here? Are the hairs on the back of her neck standing up? Does she have that prickly feeling you get when you think someone is staring at you? Will she close her locker door and meet my eyes?

If she does, then what?

I wait. I ask myself, What did you expect?

Chapter Three

This is what I remember.

I am holding the note in my hand and thinking, No way, this can't be true. Then I think, But it has to be. I know that handwriting. I know that signature. It *is* true. Now all I have to do is forget how nervous I am and follow what it says. I tell myself that Cinderella was probably nervous about going to that ball.

But she went anyway. Her heart probably fluttered when the prince saw her and made his way over to her to ask her to dance. But she danced anyway.

I'm no Cinderella, and John is no prince. He's just John, the guy I've been crazy about ever since I can remember. The guy who just got cuter and more popular year after year and who never once seemed to notice that I was anything but the daughter of his mom's curling partner until, well, until he looked at me from across the room and smiled.

At *me*.

Later, he asked if he could borrow my notes after he'd missed class for a dentist's appointment. *My* notes, not Kayla's or Jen's or Shayna's. All of this happened after he and Kayla broke up.

And then…I couldn't believe it was happening, but it was. The doorbell rang, and I opened it, and it was John.

He had a measuring cup in his hand. When he saw it was me, not my mother, he smiled again and said, *Addie*, as if he were surprised—pleasantly surprised. His mom had sent him over to borrow a cup of milk, but it took him forever to get around to telling me that. Instead he asked me if I had any plans for spring break and said he had been planning to go away for a week, but that was before he broke up with Kayla and now he wasn't sure what he was going to do. It wasn't until his mother shouted from his house across the street to ask what was taking so long that he seemed to remember what he had come for. His face turned red, and he spluttered a little. I gave him the milk and he hurried home.

The next thing I knew, there was a note on my locker.

It was from him.

From John.

It asked me to meet him.

So, feeling like Cinderella and with butterflies in my stomach, there I am, clutching the note and walking away from school. I glance around, wondering if anyone is watching. For once, I *want* someone to be watching. But no one is. And even if they were, even if the whole school were staring at me, no one would have any idea what I was doing or where I was going, because I haven't told anyone. I wish I could. I want everyone to know that Addie Murch is on her way to meet John Branksome, at his request. I especially want Jen and Shayna to know. And double especially, Kayla.

But there is no one around.

That doesn't stop me from strutting like one of those boys who wants everyone to know how cool he is. I strut across the schoolyard. I strut through the gap in the fence. I strut along the rocky little path that leads through the woods, past the new subdivision and out into the conservation area. I keep right on strutting as I follow the path to where it forks and goes deeper into the bush, taking you, if you follow it far enough, to where kids hang out for parties. I strut past the party zone and the big blackened circle with burned wood in the center, and cinder blocks and tree stumps all around it, where kids sit and drink or make out or whatever they do at their parties. I keep going, glancing at the note to make sure I haven't taken a wrong turn.

I find myself in the smallest clearing I have ever seen. It's as if someone planted a ring of trees in a tiny circle, and I'm standing in the middle of them, listening, waiting, breathing hard from all the strutting.

That's when it happens.

Twigs snap. Something rushes at me. Something is pulled down over my head, covering my eyes, my nose, my mouth, my ears. When I open my mouth to scream, whatever is blanketing my head gets sucked into my mouth. I panic and fight for breath. The material closes around my nostrils too. I am suffocating. When I start to raise my arms to rip the bag or material from my head, someone clamps my arms to my sides. I try to break free, but I'm being held too tightly.

I flash back on the rumors swirling around school the past few days. Kids have been saying that a weird guy is lurking out here. I overheard two girls talking about it in the washroom. One of them said a man had followed her and creeped her out, and that she's lucky he didn't catch her. She said she was never going to come out here again, it didn't matter who was having a party. The other one said she'd heard the police were searching for the guy because there had been so many reports, but that so far they hadn't found anything.

I am cold all over, and not from the temperature.

Someone is holding me. Someone is smothering me. Someone is stopping me from screaming.

And the whole way out here, I haven't seen another soul.

Not one single person.

I am alone in the middle of nowhere.

With a stranger.

I keep struggling, but it doesn't do me any good.

I thrash around, trying to find some way to tell whoever is there that I am going to suffocate. But I can't speak. I can't move. I can't breathe.

I feel as if I'm going to black out.

My knees buckle.

I try to stop myself from falling.

I tell myself that if I fall, whoever is out there will have won.

He will be able to do whatever he wants with me.

I wonder if anyone will find me.

Of course someone will—eventually. Because eventually someone will come out here to party. Or to walk in the woods. Or to hunt. Or something. And they will stumble on something. A shallow grave. My grave.

I try again to break free.

Instead I feel myself being lifted off the ground.

Whoever he is, he is strong. I imagine him—a hulking man, bearded, filthy clothes, boots, maybe a bush jacket, jeans, flannel shirt, hunting hat. Maybe with a hunting knife. Maybe with a gun. The girl in the bathroom, the one who said she was followed, also said she never saw him clearly. She just saw flashes of red flannel every now and then, and that's how she knew he was trailing her.

I kick. I try to scream, but when I breathe in, material—I think it's burlap—fills my mouth and everything goes black.

The next thing I remember, I am still being carried. I hear a murmur. A voice. More than one voice. Two? Three? I can't tell.

But I am definitely being carried. I am being carried down something—maybe down some stairs. Or down a hill.

Suddenly it's colder than it was before.

I hear a creaking sound.

Then I am dropped.

I hit the ground. I hear the creaking sound again. Then a bang.

It takes me a few moments to realize that my hands are not tied. I lift them to my head, and I pull off whatever is covering my head and face. I still can't see. I panic. Am I blind?

I reach out, gingerly. I have no idea where I am or what I might touch in this blackness.

I touch rock.

I touch wood.

I walk my hand up the wood and touch a latch.

A door latch. I try it. It doesn't give.

I'm inside a room. From what I remember and from the dankness I feel, I guess it's a cellar. But what cellar? The last I remember, I was out in the bush. I don't know of any houses out here. I don't even know of any abandoned cabins or shacks. But I don't spend as much time in the bush as most of the kids I know. I don't come out here on weekends to party. I've never been out here with a boy. It's never been my thing.

I think again about the creepy guy who's supposedly lurking out here, the one I overhead that girl talking about. Maybe this is his place. Or maybe he's been squatting here and has been waiting patiently for someone to stumble into his territory. Someone like me. Now he's caught me and I am in this cellar—and nobody knows where I am.

Nobody except John.

Is he out there somewhere waiting for me? Is he looking for me? Did he see or hear something? Is he close by?

Is he too close?

What if the guy who grabbed me has seen him? What if he managed to sneak up on John and used his hunting knife to…to get rid of John?

Oh my god.

Or…

What if John thinks I didn't show up?

What if he thinks I ignored his note, and he's given up on me and is on his way back home? Or maybe he's there already. I realize I have no idea how much time has passed, how long I've been here, whether it's dark outside or light. I just don't know.

All I know is that I'm in this room, behind this door, and that on the other side is the person who grabbed me and carried me here and who is now preparing to…to do something with me.

I feel like I'm going to throw up.

I hear a sound, a click. Is he out there? I wait. Nothing happens.

I fight to keep calm. To steady my nerves.

I touch the door again. I touch the latch. I wrap my fingers around it, catch my breath and push down.

The latch gives.

But what if he's out there? What if he's sharpening his knife or preparing… to do whatever it is he intends to do?

I hesitate.

I don't want to stay here. But what if this side of the door is safer than the other side?

If it is, it won't be forever. The minute he decides to open that door, I stop being safe. I have to get away. I have no choice. I have to open the door and run.

My whole body is shaking. I draw in a deep breath and whisper one word to myself. *Courage.* Then I push.

I push the door open and take off like a sprinter, shooting out of the small room and into impenetrable darkness. Panic rises in my throat. Where am I? Which way do I run? Where is out?

Where is he?

My eyes adjust a little. I see shapes. Are those stairs over there? Is that a sliver of light above?

I race for the tiny gash of brightness. They *are* stairs. They're made of stone, and they're narrow and steep. I race toward them.

A shape comes at me.

A huge blacker-than-black shape, bigger than any man I have ever seen. It zooms toward me and is about to engulf me.

I scream.

I scream and scream and scream as I flail at the thing with both hands, trying to beat it away from me. I am screaming as I stumble and fall.

I force myself to my feet again, still screaming. I feel wetness—I've peed myself.

Something flashes, brighter than a thousand lightning bolts, completely blinding me.

After the flash, the whole cellar goes black again. It's blacker than ever now. My eyes can no longer make out anything. Every hair on my body stands up. I hear breathing. Is it me or him?

Something touches me.

Some*one* touches me.

I scream again.

Chapter Four

I'm still screaming when, as if a switch
has been thrown, the darkness is
replaced by brilliant light.

I'm still screaming as my eyes
adjust again, this time to being able to
see, and I realize that the shape I've
been fighting off, that large mass of evil
blackness, is a person in a cape, his arms
up over his head.

I see a hand. It's a girl's hand.

There are more shapes. More people. They're all dressed in black and all wearing masks. All except the person holding a light. That person is wearing a hat and a wig, but she hasn't hidden her face. She's holding the light high above a camera on a tripod.

Camera.

There's a masked person behind the camera. I am being filmed.

It takes longer than I like to admit before I stop screaming. Then I just stand there with my mouth hanging open, staring at all the masks. I have no idea what I'm thinking. I've looked at those pictures of myself, that footage, maybe a thousand times since then, and I still have no idea what I was thinking. I look at myself, at my open mouth and my wide eyes, at my heaving chest, at the look of terror on my face, and I can't remember what was going through my mind.

Maybe nothing. Maybe that was my brain's way of protecting me— it blocked off all my thoughts.

And then it comes. The part where I turn and run up the stairs.

Or *try* to.

Because I trip and fall and let out an unworldly sound. That's when everyone laughs. I pick myself up, and, arms waving like a wild thing, legs pumping, I fly up the stairs. At the top there is nothing but a floor surrounded by scrubby trees and bush, which is why I've never seen this place before, because all that's left of it is underground. I hear muffled laughter behind me. I run. I keep on running. I don't even realize until later that the person I pass as I run is John. I think he calls my name. Or maybe I imagine that. But I don't stop. I run until I am out of the bush and back behind the school. Then I run home, to my backyard, to the space under the back porch. I crawl under there just like I used to when I was little, and I curl up and cry.

The whole time I'm under there, I think about how scared I was. Terrified. I thought some maniac had grabbed me. I thought he was going to kill me. I thought I was going to die.

Now I don't know if all that stuff I heard about a man out in the bush was even true. Maybe those girls said what they said because they wanted me to hear it. Maybe they planned it.

Because there is no doubt in my mind that the whole thing was planned. Why else would there have been so many people in that cellar? Why would there have been a camera? Why so much laughter? This was someone's idea of a joke.

Then I think, What did I ever do to deserve something like that?

I think, How could anyone pull a prank like that? What's so funny about scaring someone almost to death?

I wonder if John was involved. Did he leave that note to lure me out there?

But he wasn't in the cellar with the rest of them. I remember now that I ran past him when I finally escaped. I remember that when he looked at me, he had a puzzled expression on his face, as if he didn't know what was going on.

Still, I wouldn't have been out there if it wasn't for his note.

There's something else.

There were a lot of people there. One of them—the one without a mask—was Neely.

My former best friend Neely.

I can't decide if that hurts more than thinking John may have been involved. What did I ever do to Neely to make her want to pull a practical joke like that?

By now, everyone knows. While I'm curled up in a little ball under my porch, crying like a baby, everyone is probably talking about what happened out there. Everyone is having a good laugh at my expense. It's not just the kids who were out there. By now, they will have told everyone they know.

And then there is the camera.

Someone was recording the whole thing.

I have no idea what time it is when I finally stop crying. By then I have completely dehydrated myself. I couldn't shed another tear even if I wanted to. But I stay where I am, even though it's getting dark. I squeeze my eyes shut, and I see Neely's face. The light flashed in my eyes, I heard laughing, and the next thing I knew, I was staring at Neely, holding that light so the whole thing could be recorded. She used to be my best friend, so she knows everything there is to know about me. She knows things my family doesn't even know. She knows things I would never tell anyone else.

Has *she*? Has she told people my secrets?

Was she behind what happened?

She's the only person who knows for a fact—because I told her—that I've had a crush on John for as long as I can remember. Now I wonder if John really wrote that note and stuck it in my locker or if Neely did. But if John didn't write the note, what was he doing out there, not with everyone else, but outside? Why did he look so puzzled when I ran by?

After a while, I hear a voice. It's my mother. She's calling me in a sing-song voice that I haven't heard since I was a kid, when Neely and I used to play outside until dark and our mothers would open their doors and call us to come home. My mom hasn't done that since I got my first cell phone. She doesn't have to. She phones me or texts me and asks where I am and tells me to get home.

But my cell phone isn't on.

I listen to her calling me. I don't think I imagine the worry in her voice. I roll out from under the porch and brush myself off.

"Coming!" I call. I wipe my face as best I can, but as soon as I step into the kitchen, my mother stops what she's doing and stares at me.

"What happened to your face?" she asks. Her eyes drop down a few inches. "What happened to your jacket?"

I start to say, "Nothing." But, like a baby, I start crying. Once I start, I can't stop.

She asks me again. "Addie, what's wrong?"

I still don't tell her. How can I? How can I tell my mother I'm such a loser that my best friend and a bunch of her friends ganged up on me with this joke and that I wasn't a good sport, and I didn't find it funny? I didn't laugh along with everyone else. Instead I freaked out, which makes me an even bigger loser than I was when I got out of bed this morning.

I tell my mom that I tripped over something on the way home from school and that's how my jacket got so dirty. I get changed. I set the table like I do every night, as if nothing has happened. I poke at my peas and potatoes and meat, but by then it doesn't matter, because my dad has come home and he's talking excitedly about a big sale he's just landed that's going to make him top guy at the dealership again this year. My dad sells agricultural implements and, lately, recreational vehicles. *You go where the money is*, my dad says. *Then you make people want what you're selling*. My dad can make anyone want anything.

That's the thing no one understands. My dad is the most talkative guy on the planet. Me, I'm tongue-tied and shy, always afraid that if anyone looks too closely at me, they'll find out what a loser I really am. I can't help it. I've been like this my whole life. When I started high school, it got worse.

My high school is huge compared to my elementary school. Kids from six different schools in six different towns go to my high school, including some kids from Lake Haven, which used to be a nothing town but is now one of the hottest places around for what they call "estate housing." Rich people have built big houses on all the lakes up there. Their kids go to my high school. Some of them, especially the girls, think they're better than everyone else. Some of them get off on giving other people a hard time. For some reason, they decided to pick on me. And for some reason, Neely, who used to be my best friend, decided she wanted to get in with those girls. Kayla, Jen and Shayna are from Lake Haven.

Anyway, lucky for me, my dad's so excited about the sale that neither he nor my mom notices I haven't eaten a thing.

I go up to my room and try to do my homework. I give up when I realize that I don't care about algebra tonight. Instead, I log in to my computer and check my email. Don't ask me why— I hardly get any anymore.

But there's something in my inbox. I can't tell who it's from, but I check it anyway.

It's from Anonymous. There's a picture right there in the email screen.

A picture of me, wide-eyed and screaming. Underneath is a link. My hand shakes when I click on it.

When I watch the video the link takes me to, I almost stop breathing. When it's over, I watch it again. And again. I don't know how many times I watch it. A lot.

Sometime later that night, I start crying again, only this time I really can't stop.

Chapter Five

No one is home the next morning when I get dressed for school. My dad always leaves early, hours before the first customer is out of bed, and it's my mom's day to volunteer at the church. So there's just me.

I skip breakfast. I'm not hungry.

I walk to school and almost turn back half a dozen times.

I think about the video and wonder if everyone has seen it by now.

When the school comes into sight, my question is answered. A girl spots me. She nudges the girl next to her, who nudges the girl next to her. They all stare at me. One of them says something to the other two. I can't hear what they say, but I can see them. They're laughing.

Someone else hears them and turns to see what's so funny. There are maybe fifteen or twenty kids hanging around outside the school, and pretty soon they're all looking at me and laughing.

My stomach does acrobatics. I'm glad I didn't have breakfast, because if I had, it would be on the ground right now.

I slow to a stop. Part of me—okay, all of me—wants to run home and hide under my bed and never come out again. But I'm not stupid. I know hiding doesn't solve anything, ever. Sooner or later, you have to come out. So I keep walking. My legs are as shaky as a newborn deer's. My eyes are stinging. My throat is tight and dry. But I keep going. I tell myself I can get through this. I even believe it until I get inside and start what seems like the longest walk of my life— up the stairs to the second floor and down the east hallway, which is crowded with kids, all the way to the end where my locker is.

You'd think the queen was going by.

Or a death-row prisoner on the way to his execution.

With every step I take, another couple of kids fall silent, until finally the crowded hall is like a cemetery filled with mourners, that's how quiet it is.

I pretend not to notice. I don't dare look at any of the faces that are looking at me. I take hold of my lock and start to work the combination.

I open my locker.

There, on the inside of the locker door, where my mirror should be, is a poster-sized picture of my face, mouth wide open, eyes wide open, in a silent scream of terror.

Someone laughs. It's one of the kids near my locker.

More kids laugh, because what happened to me is the funniest thing that's ever happened here. Because it's hilarious to see someone who's convinced she's about to be strangled or hacked to death by some creepy stranger who hangs out in the bush.

I reach for the poster.

I rip it from the door.

I tear it into a thousand pieces.

I flee to the girls' bathroom and lock myself in a stall.

I stay there after the bell has rung.

I stay there even when I hear the click of heels on the tile floor outside.

"Addie? Addie, are you in there?" It's Ms. LaPointe. She knocks on the door of the stall. "Addie, I heard what happened. Come out, and we'll go down to the office and talk about it."

By then my eyes are swollen to three times their normal size, and I can barely see out of them. My cheeks are wet with tears, my nose is red from blowing, and my head is aching, probably from dehydration.

"Addie?" She sounds tense, as if she's afraid what I might be doing in there. "Addie, if you don't come out, I'll have to get Mr. Sloane to open the door."

Mr. Sloane is head of maintenance. I imagine *that* getting around— Mr. Sloane went into the girls' bathroom with his toolbox, and a crying you-know-who comes out with Ms. LaPointe. I open the stall door.

Ms. LaPointe looks as concerned as any vice-principal would under the circumstances. She also looks relieved as she checks out my wrists and scans me for any other signs of self-damage.

"I heard what happened," she says again. "Let's go to the office and talk."

I agree because I can't think of any other place in the school I want to go to or that you could get me to go to. But I don't want to talk.

The halls are quiet, and most of the classroom doors are closed. A couple of kids glance through the few that are open as we go by, but their faces are expressionless. Maybe they're the only ones in school who don't know what happened. Or maybe they don't care.

Ms. LaPointe ushers me into her tiny office and closes the door. She pulls down the blinds on the window that looks out into the main office.

"Now, then," she says when we are both seated. "What do you want to do about this situation, Addie?"

What do I want to do?

"What do you mean?"

"I know about the video," she says. "I also know that someone—I don't know who or how—got hold of the school email list and sent the link to everyone on it."

Everyone in the whole school got the same link I did? I feel like throwing up.

"So even though the incident—"

Incident—that's school language for what happened to me. It's a nice, neutral word.

"—didn't take place on school property, we can still notify the police about our computer system being hacked. We can get them to investigate. When they find out who did it, we can lay charges against that person—or persons."

"For hacking the school computer," I say. It's not a question. I'm just trying to understand how the school computer system and what happened to it is more important than what happened to me.

"I think *you* should talk to the police about the incident, Addie. Maybe with your parents."

My parents still have no idea what's going on.

"I'm not a lawyer. What I do know about the law is pretty much confined to what happens here at school. But there may be some charge that you can press, something that you can do. That is, if you want to."

Maybe I read too much into her expression and the tone of her voice, but it seems to me Ms. LaPointe knows more than she's letting on. She knows there's no law against the kind of practical joke that was played on me. I wasn't physically hurt. I wasn't actually kidnapped. I wasn't forcibly confined—the door in the cellar turned out not to be locked. It was all just good fun—for the jokers.

I look at Ms. LaPointe's desk, not at Ms. LaPointe, and think about what to do. Some people would probably have laughed at the joke along with everyone else and then moved on. But a person like that would have to believe that he or she was the target of a truly funny practical joke—no harm, no foul. I don't believe that. I wish I did. I wish I could shrug the whole thing off. But I keep thinking that someone—more than one someone— planned and executed a so-called joke that was intended not only to scare me to death but also to create an online video to show to everyone in my school. Someone wanted everyone to laugh at me. And laughter isn't always funny. Sometimes it cuts like a knife.

I stand up. I say, "I'm going home." I leave without stopping at my locker. When I get home, I crawl into bed. I'm still in bed when my mother gets back from the church, but she doesn't know I'm there. She doesn't find out until suppertime, when she's worried about me and comes into my room to look at my calendar to see if I have any after-school events. By then, so they tell me, I've cried myself out, I have no appetite, and all I see is darkness.

Chapter Six

It turns out Ms. LaPointe called my
parents that night. It turns out my parents
then watched the video and called the
police. It turns out the police told them
that no law had been broken, but that they
were making every effort to ascertain
(cop talk) whether the school computer
system had been hacked. If so, they said

they would pursue the perpetrator with the full force of the law.

"I can't believe they're going to let those kids get away with what they did," my mother says, not to me, but to my father and at the top of her lungs. She's furious.

"Poor Addie," my dad says. "I've been hoping she would break out of that shell. Then maybe this never would have happened."

"You think this is *her* fault?" my mom asks.

"No, of course not. But, Leslie, you know things are a lot easier for kids who aren't so thin-skinned, who don't analyze every move they make or think that every decision is a matter of life and death."

I hear my mother sigh.

I don't sleep that night. The next morning, I refuse to go to school. My mom doesn't argue with me.

I stay in bed, my eyes glued to my cell phone, waiting for John to call, waiting for Neely to call. I'm not sure which call I wish for more.

Neely is my best friend.

Correction. Neely was my best friend up until the beginning of this school year. But Neely was there, holding that light. She didn't just see what they did to me. She was involved.

She doesn't call.

John does. He swears he had nothing to do with what happened. He says Kayla asked to meet him. I don't know whether to believe him or not. He doesn't call again.

I don't know how many days pass after that. All I know is that one morning when there's no one in the house, I go to the bathroom, find a brand-new bottle of aspirin and swallow the whole thing. About an hour later, I panic. I call my mom and tell her what I did. I spend the next two days locked down in the regional hospital, where they monitor my blood levels and where a doctor says, "Maybe you think life sucks, but let me tell you, young lady, life on dialysis sucks a lot more." It turns out I could have wiped out my kidneys without taking myself with them.

They make me talk to a shrink before they let me go home. Then I have to go regularly and talk to another one. I lose fifteen pounds. I can't sleep. I don't care about food. I don't care about anything. I don't think I even realize that I don't care.

Neely doesn't call.

Christmas comes and goes. And then—I don't know if it's the medication or if it's that a new year has rolled around—I decide to go back to school.

Crazy, huh?

So here I am, back.

And there she is, just like always. Except for the fact that she's avoiding me, she's acting like nothing happened.

I still can't believe what she did. I still have no idea why she did it. Sure, I get that she didn't want to be friends with me anymore. She couldn't have made it any clearer. But to do something like that? To humiliate me in front of all those kids just to prove she's cool? To hack the school computer the way she did, email that link to every kid in school to make sure they saw it, post that video so people all over the world could get a good laugh? That's hard-core. What did I do to deserve that?

I stand there. I look at the kids who are looking at Neely—and at me. I wait. But she doesn't even glance in my direction. She doesn't acknowledge me. Instead she backs out of her locker and slams the door. She keeps her head down as she threads her lock through the locker loops and fastens it. She turns away from me and walks down the hall. I watch her merge with the mass of other kids until all I see is the back of her head, until she is swallowed up altogether. Then I turn. I walk in the opposite direction, down the hall, down the stairs, past the office and out the big front doors. I am done here. I am never coming back. Why should I?

Neely's Story

Chapter Seven

There's no such thing as a free lunch.
My dad must have said that a million
times. That, and *You pay now or you
pay later, but you always pay*. My mom
says he's cynical. She says he thinks
everyone has an angle. Everyone wants
something. That's where the paying
comes in. One way or another, you have
to pay the price for everything you get

in this life. He says once you know that, you know all there is to know.

Me, I've always thought, sure, you have to pay for things. It makes sense, right? And if you're smart, you know that you get what you pay for, so you're careful, you go for quality. Right?

The thing I've always wanted, my big-ticket item, is change. You would too, if you were me.

I grew up in this town. I went to the same kindergarten as every other kid here. I went to the same elementary school too, the same one as Addie. We didn't have any choice. If you live anywhere in Monroe Township, you go to Monroe Elementary—unless your parents send you to a faith-based school. Our parents didn't.

Addie and I met in first grade when we were assigned to the same table at the front of the class. We were both shy. I live on a farm outside of town, and up until kindergarten, I spent almost all my time at home. My playmates were mostly my cousins. Three of them live in a house on our property, along with my aunt, who has multiple sclerosis, and my uncle. Four more live down the road on another farm. I have another aunt and uncle who live ten miles away, in another township. And that's just on my mom's side of the family. My dad has five brothers. Three of them are farmers like my dad, one is a veterinarian and one is a surgeon. All but one of them live close by, they're all married, and they all have kids. All my cousins are older than me.

Maybe because I'm the youngest by a couple of years and got shut out of a lot of activities, I've always been shy. By the time I got to grade one, I'd been asked a thousand times if the cat had got my tongue. After that I was teased for being afraid of my own shadow.

It wasn't all that long ago that my mother told me she'd been worried about me back then. She'd thought I had a hearing problem or maybe some kind of disability. That's how quiet I was. Like Addie.

Addie has a brother, but he's ten years older than her and has been away at school since she was in second grade. He's some kind of science genius and has almost finished his PhD. Both of Addie's parents were only children. All four of her grandparents died before she got to elementary school, two in a car accident, one of a heart attack and one of cancer. Her family is as tiny as mine is huge. But for some reason, we hit it off right away.

Addie was—still is—as quiet as I was. She was—is—much shyer. Even when she was little, she wore her bangs long so that they hung over her eyes, like a curtain. Our second-grade teacher once brought a barrette to school and pinned her hair back. *So I can see the girl under there*, she said. Everyone laughed at that—everyone except Addie. You know how some people are afraid of snakes? Or the dark? Or whatever it is they imagine is hiding at the back of the closet?

Well, Addie is afraid of people. She's afraid they're watching her and measuring her and finding fault with her.

She's deathly afraid of being teased or laughed at.

But we were buddies. Until we got to high school.

The high school is a comprehensive located in Monroe. Kids from six different elementary schools get bused in. In grade nine, for the first time ever, I found myself in classes with kids I had never met before. Addie was nervous about that. She spent the whole week before school started freaking out that she and I might have different timetables and not be in all the same classes. That didn't bother me.

Confession—I was hoping we wouldn't be in *any* classes together.

Sounds mean, huh? Especially since I just said she was my best friend all through elementary school. But that started to change. It changed for good because of something one of my cousins said to me while I was visiting Boston—her father is the surgeon. She wanted to take me to a party, and I didn't want to go because I didn't know what I would say to complete strangers and because I was sure no one would like me.

She looked at me and said, "You're my cousin, Neely. But I have to tell you this. I used to think you always acted kind of superior, like you thought you were better than everyone else."

"Me?" You could have knocked me over with a feather, as my grandpa would have said.

"You never joined in. You always said you had something else to do. You'd just sit there and watch. People thought you were stuck up. If you hang back all the time, what are they supposed to think? You should start worrying more about how the other person feels and less about yourself."

Was she kidding? All I ever thought about was the other person. Does she like me? Does he think I'm a dweeb? Why doesn't she talk to me?

"You can't wait for the other person all the time," my cousin said. "You have to include them if you want them to include you. You can't make everyone else do the heavy lifting."

The way she said it, it was like she was accusing me of something, like being self-centered. So I did what I usually did when I thought someone was criticizing me—I started to cry.

Which led to a massive heart-to-heart with my cousin.

Which led to her giving me some tips.

Which led to me vowing to change.

Which meant making a huge effort to forget my own nervousness and concentrate instead on trying to put other people at ease.

Which led to my taking some initiative at the party, even though I was sure I was going to throw up.

Which led to my meeting a nice guy.

And his friends.

And having fun.

All of which led to my promising myself that when I got home, I would be a brand-new Neely.

Chapter Eight

I tried to bring Addie along with me. Really, I did.

But she was too scared to even try most of the time. So I had to go it alone.

It hasn't been easy, despite what Addie thinks. She's made it a lot harder by the way she acts.

In grade nine, we were in most of the same classes. But this year is different.

This year we aren't in the same home-room. We aren't in the same French, history or civics classes either. But Addie is in my English and math classes, where on the first day she made sure to grab the seat next to mine. She's also in my gym class, where she sticks to me like glue.

Here's what I discovered last year. In the classes where it was just me and not Addie too, I could be anyone I wanted. Most of the kids didn't know me, because most of them came from other schools. In fact, most of them didn't know most of the other kids either. That meant I could put into practice what I'd learned in Boston. I made plenty of friends in those classes. I'm doing even better this year.

But in the classes where Addie clings to me, it's harder. She sucks up my time and energy. She never wants to talk to anyone else—she's convinced they won't like her. When we have to break into groups, she stays silent. She hides behind her hair. Now I see how shy she really is. It's like a disease with her. She can't seem to shake it off. I've been trying to help her. Her answer every time? "I can't. I'll just die if I have to." It doesn't do any good to tell her that it's medically impossible for anyone to die of shyness. Or embarrassment. Or being laughed at, for that matter.

At the urging of my English teacher—and to my surprise—I decided to try out for the school play this year. I tried to get Addie to audition too, but she wouldn't. So then I tried to get her into doing costumes or sets or something. But she wouldn't do that either. And, if you ask me, she tried to undermine my confidence by telling me all the time how the popular kids would get the parts, not kids like "us." It made me

mad because I don't think I'm like her.
Not anymore.

I showed her. I got a part. Not a
starring role, but not a walk-on either. I
got to play the best friend of the female
lead. That's how I got to know Jen and
Kayla and Shayna. Kayla landed the
female lead. She was good. She was
nice too. At least, I thought she was. And
I wasn't the only one. John felt the same
way. That's John Branksome, the cutest
guy in school. The most athletic. The
boy who was always picked for whatever production was put on. Everyone
likes John. Teachers adore him. Kayla
fell for him. They hung together for
a while. Then it was over—at least, it
was over as far as John was concerned.
To tell the truth, I don't know whether
John was really into a relationship or
if it was all Kayla. All I know is what
happened next.

Chapter Nine

"Your little friend is staring at you again." That's Kayla. She's talking about Addie, who she insists on calling my "little friend." It bugs me, but I don't know how to make her stop without also causing her to freeze me out.

We're sitting in the cafeteria. "We" are Kayla, Jen, Shayna and me. The three of them went to different elementary schools, but they knew each other because they were in the same gymnastics club. They're all pretty and all skinny, like you'd expect gymnasts to be. They're the most popular girls in grade ten, and you just know that when the time comes, one of them is going to be prom queen.

For some reason I don't understand, Kayla has a real hate on for Addie. She makes snide remarks about her all the time, about how big her nose is (it's not that big), how she slouches all the time (that's true—Addie always seems to be collapsing in on herself, as if all she wants is to disappear), how tacky her clothes are (Addie doesn't make much of an effort to keep up to date) and how she's so quiet all the time. Jen says Addie reminds her of Boo Radley, the character from *To Kill a Mockingbird* who you never see and who everyone regards as some kind of ghost.

"She's nothing like Boo Radley," I say. I glance at Addie and see right away that I am wrong. She's exactly like him—pale, invisible to most people and happiest when she's in the shadows, unseen. And Kayla's right—she is staring at me.

I shake my head at her and don't even try to hide my annoyance. Confession—I wish Addie would leave me alone. I'm not like her anymore. I've moved on.

"She is too," Jen says. "She's a female Boo Radley—quiet and creepy." She nudges Kayla, and they look at Addie again, only now Addie isn't alone. John Branksome is standing beside her, handing her something and smiling at her.

"What the—" Kayla splutters.

I know what's going on because Addie told me. John borrowed her history notes to copy. John lives across the street from her. His mom and Addie's mom are friends. John and Addie have known each other practically since the day she was born. But I don't tell Kayla that, not when she's being such a bitch.

Instead I say, "Yeah, he's been over at her house a lot lately."

"Lately?"

"You know, since the play."

After the play was over, just about the time Kayla was crowing to everyone about her "new boyfriend," John dumped her. That's assuming he was ever with her. It still isn't clear to me. Kayla acted like they were a couple. John, not so much. Sometimes it seemed to me that they were just in a play together.

"He hangs out with her?" Kayla says, still with plenty of splutter.

"Forget it," Shayna says. "Forget him. If he's interested in her, he's a loser."

This earns her evil eyes from both Kayla and Jen. Maybe I'm wrong, but just the thought that she might have been hanging out with someone who one her friends is now calling a loser seems to get Kayla all riled up.

"What do you know?" Jen says. Jen is Kayla's best friend. She sticks up for Kayla no matter what. "He probably just feels sorry for her. I know I do."

"Yeah," says Kayla, practically choking on the word. "Yeah, that's probably it." But she can't take her eyes off them. When John squeezes Addie's arm and Addie responds by staring adoringly up at him, Kayla goes pale.

"Addie's always had a thing for him," I say. I'd like to tell you I say it simply because it happens to be true. But really, I say it because I want to make a dig at Addie, just like I made one at Kayla. The truth is, they're both getting on my nerves.

"So you know John, right?" Kayla says.

"Yeah."

"Then talk to him for me." It comes out like a command.

"And tell him what?"

"Tell him to call me. Tell him I'm sorry for whatever I did. Tell him I want him back."

"Right," I say. It comes out the way it would if I were talking to Addie, and not at all the way I've been talking to Kayla, the suck-up way you more or less have to talk to Kayla. "What good would that do? He's already made up his mind."

"Says who?" Shayna demands.

"He wants that worm instead?" Jen says. "You can't be serious!"

"I just meant—"

"We know what you meant," Shayna says.

Kayla looks at me with her bitchy queen look, the one that lets everyone know she is not pleased. Kayla's parents are divorced, and Kayla lives with her mother in a massive house in what used to be a nothing town. Now it's filled with the massive houses of rich people who love all the lakes, especially if they can have the only property on one of them. Kayla's mom "dabbles" (Kayla's word) in interior design for these people. Her dad owns a bunch of companies and makes sure Kayla gets everything she wants and then some. Kayla says he's not nearly so generous with her mom and that she's pretty sure he pampers his princess (that's what her dad supposedly calls her) as a way of getting back at his ex-wife. Kayla says it's the best possible position for her to be in—both of her parents are always competing for her loyalty.

Because she's a princess, I'm sure she's going to say something bitchy to me. But she doesn't. She gazes across the table at Addie with a thoughtful expression on her face. Addie doesn't notice. She is alone now, her nose in a book. If I know her, she's trying hard to hide herself in its pages.

Chapter Ten

"Mom," I call as I come through the door the following week. "I'm home."

My mom pokes her head out of the kitchen. She looks surprised to see I'm not alone. Kayla, Shayna and Jen are with me. I introduce them. They sound polite enough when they greet her, but there's something snotty in their voices and in the way they gaze around, taking in the furniture we've had forever, the framed needlework on the walls that my mother is so proud of, the wear marks on the floor. I've never been to their houses, but something tells me everything in them is newer and shinier and more expensive.

"We're going up to my room," I say.

"I'll bring you some lemonade and cookies," my mom says. "I made them this afternoon."

Kayla makes a big fuss about that, telling my mother how she'd love a homemade cookie because her mother is always far too busy to cook, and anyway she's not very good at it because when she was married and they were living with her dad, they had a house-keeper who took care of all that. Now my mom makes a big fuss.

"Imagine that! I could use some help around here."

"I'm sure you could," Kayla says, smiling.

Up we go to my room, which suddenly seems too small and too shabby. My mom appears a few minutes later with a tray. She passes it around as if she's a maid. She beams when Kayla nibbles a cookie and pronounces it "divine."

We're sitting on the bed and the floor, and Kayla's on my desk chair. The talk is halfhearted and jumps around. Then Kayla glances at the computer on my desk and says, "Oh my god."

Jen and Shayna turn to look at her. They always do when Kayla seems upset about something.

"The spring review," Kayla says. "I forgot." She glances horror-stricken at Jen.

The high school does a review every year. You have to try out to be in it.

"I'm supposed to get the word out about auditions."

Jen looks up at the computer. "I bet Neely won't mind if you use her computer."

I shrug. "Go ahead."

"You do it, Jen," Kayla says. "You're the computer nerd."

It's true. Jen's dad is a hot-shot programmer. He worked for years in Silicon Valley. Now he consults from home, another big house up near where Kayla lives. I doubt Kayla would admit it, but I've heard that Jen's parents are even richer than Kayla's.

Jen changes places with Kayla. While she starts tapping away on the keyboard and clicking with the mouse, Kayla tells us what she's thinking of doing for the review. She asks me about the kids I know, whether any of them have any special talents. She reaches for another cookie. She seems nice now, like a normal person. When suppertime rolls around and the three of them get ready to go, Kayla stops by the kitchen to thank my mother and to ask for her cookie recipe. My mother promises to send it to school with me the next day. She sounds pleased.

"It's nice to see you bring home friends again," she says later. She's at the kitchen table, writing neatly on a recipe card that has a gingham border. "You should invite them back again."

Chapter Eleven

Two days later, I'm looking around the cafeteria. I see Kayla sitting by herself at a table near the back, and I make my way toward her. She's bent over the table, hard in concentration as she copies something from a paper in front of her.

"Hey," I say.

She almost jumps out of her chair.

"Are you trying to give me a heart attack?" She grabs the paper she was copying and jams it into her pocket. I see that it's a note of some kind, but I have no idea who wrote it or what it's about. She's also flipped her notebook shut. Whatever she's been doing, she doesn't want me to know about it.

"Well, you might as well sit down," she says, sweeping the notebook into her bag.

I sit, and pretty soon the rest of the gang is there. Kayla relaxes.

"So," Jen says, "what about the movie?"

"Movie?" I say. "What movie?"

"Shayna wants to make another movie," Kayla says. "She's made a bunch of them."

"Really?" This is news to me. It also suggests that there is more to Shayna than I suspected. "What kind of movies?"

"All kinds," Kayla says, answering for her. "But this one is going to be a horror movie, right, Shayn?"

Shayna nods.

"You want to be in it?" Kayla asks.

"Me?" I glance at Shayna. "You want *me* in your movie?"

Kayla answers again. "We're all going to be in it. What do you say?"

I say yes. I've never been in a movie before.

Kayla outlines the script. "There's a place out in the bush," she says. "Shayna's going to use that as her main location, right, Shayn?" Shayna nods. "It's going to be spooky. All dark and creepy. Tons of ambience. Right, Shayn?"

Shayna nods again, and before I know it, I have a part in a movie. Shayna finally takes over, telling us in her quiet voice what she has in mind and how important it's going to be that everyone is flexible and ready to improvise on the set. She wants to shoot after school at the end of the week. In the meantime, we need to find costumes. These are going to be mainly black. Someone—naturally, it turns out to be Kayla—has to wear a black cape and wig and a mask. She's going to be the movie's slasher.

"Every movie has to have a slasher," Kayla says, all excited. "But they're almost always guys. Shayna wants to turn the genre on its head. She wants to have a female slasher."

We talk about what we're going to wear and where we're going to get what we need. Kayla volunteers to have her mother scout out some stuff.

"She's going to a design conference tomorrow," she tells us. "She has a friend who's in the movie business. I bet she can set us up with some great stuff."

She's just as excited two days later. "You guys have to come over after school," she says. "You have to see what my mom got for us."

I could probably take the bus with them after school, but I remind Kayla that I have no way to get home afterward.

"No problem," she says. I think she's going to arrange a ride for me and that I am finally going to see her massive house. But instead she says, "I'll bring your costume to school with me. I'll make sure it's great."

She keeps her word. She brings me a black suit, black gloves, a Freddy Krueger-style hat and a black wig with long, scraggly hair.

"You're going to look so cool," she says.

Chapter Twelve

We meet after last class and go to a coffee shop near the school to have something to eat while Shayna outlines her plan for the shoot. The sun is starting to set by the time we head out to the bush on the outskirts of town where kids go to have parties, make out and just do whatever they want to do, away from adults or anyone else. We tramp over dried leaves, step over fallen trees and watch for tree roots that have broken the surface and formed hazards on the worn path. Finally Kayla says, "There it is."

I don't see anything but more bush, but Kayla leads on, walking faster now, like a horse in sight of its stable and food. As we get closer, I see that there is something here after all—a rectangular patch that looks different from the terrain surrounding it. But not until we're actually standing inside the rectangle do I see what it is—the foundation of a derelict cabin. And by derelict, I mean almost gone. All that's left of the walls is a layer of old rock. The floorboards are covered in moss and leaves. Some have holes in them, and some are missing. But this was definitely a cabin. I'm kind of surprised. I've never come out here with other kids, but you'd think I would at least have heard of this place.

Kayla leads the way to a hole in the middle of the floor that turns out to be the opening to a flight of stairs.

"It's creepy down there," she says.

Shayna grins. "It's perfect."

The three of them pull out flashlights, and Shayna leads the way down the stairs. I'm annoyed that no one told me to bring a flashlight. I stick close to Jen, who is the last one down. I'm surprised to find that there are four other kids down there, all of them boys, all of them dressed in black. I'm also surprised to hear hammering and screaming.

"What's—?"

Kayla shushes me.

"It's part of the setup," she says. "Pay attention to Shayna. She's going to tell you what to do."

Shayna lays it out in a hushed voice. She wants to film the most dramatic part of her movie first—the one that will make people gasp with fright. She sets us up around the bottom of the stairs. She says she won't need me in this particular scene—she has something special in mind for me. But for now, she needs me right beside her, holding a light above her camera so that she can get the shot she wants.

Everyone puts on masks. The hammering suddenly stops. I hear a sob. Wow, I think. It sounds great—like a real, actual, terrified sob.

I'm standing next to Shayna and her camera, holding a light high up over my head. Everyone has a mask on except me and Shayna, but she's hidden behind the camera.

All of a sudden something—no, some*one*—comes running out of the darkness. The person screams as she makes a dash for the stairs. I'm thinking this girl sounds as terrified as any real actress I have ever seen in any slasher movie.

She's racing through the darkness. Then she trips and falls on the stairs. At first I think it's an accident, but Shayna doesn't move. She's still crouched behind her camera, still shooting, so I think the girl was supposed to fall.

Someone else—Kayla—in a cape and mask and wig, throws her arms up over her head and growls like a crazed dog as she moves in, towering over the girl.

The girl looks up, and that's when I see who it is.

It's Addie.

What is Addie doing in Shayna's movie? As far as I know, the two of them have never spoken to each other. But it's definitely Addie. She screams and scrambles, trying to get to her feet. Her terror is so real, I'm amazed. I never knew she could act like that, and I wonder how Shayna knew. That has to be why she asked Addie to be in her movie.

Addie screams again. Tears are running down her face. So is snot. She shrieks as Kayla gets closer. I see something glint. A knife. Kayla has a knife.

Addie goes up the stairs on her hands and feet. She's whimpering. It's an amazing performance.

When she's halfway up, everyone starts to laugh.

Everyone except Addie.

She turns her head. Her eyes meet mine. She looks so surprised.

That's when it hits me. She isn't acting. Her terror is real.

She turns and runs. I look at Shayna. She's pointing the camera at me now.

Suddenly the whole basement gets light. Everyone has a flashlight—everyone but me—and they all turn them on. They're laughing as if they've seen the funniest thing in the whole world.

"That'll teach her," Kayla says.

The words echo in my head.

Bitch, I think.

What am I doing here?

That night I get an email from the school. There's a link to an online video. I click on it.

It's Shayna's movie.

Chapter Thirteen

The next day at school, everyone is talking about Shayna's movie. I'm with Kayla and Jen and Shayna when someone comes up to me and says, "That was some production, Neely."

I start to tell her it wasn't me, that I had nothing to do with it. But Kayla answers before I do. "She did a great job," she says. "I think that's the best practical joke I ever heard of."

"But I didn't—"

Jen jabs me in the side with her elbow. As soon as the girl dashes off, Kayla turns to me and says in a sweet voice, "Yours is the only recognizable face in that video, Neely. Except for your loser friend, of course."

"Yeah, but I didn't make that movie."

"Oh?" More sweetness. The fake type. The type that makes you want to gag. "Well, I'm pretty sure that there's no one who will back you up if you try to involve me or anyone else."

Jen and Shayna are staring at me. I know that they will never betray Kayla. They probably have an alibi all worked out. They'll deny, deny, deny. I also realize that I have no idea who any of the boys were. Or what Addie was doing in that wrecked old house. Or how they got her there.

I don't know anything.

Except that anyone who sees that video is going to see my face.

"Don't worry," Kayla says. "It's not like it's a crime."

She's right about that. It's a joke, not a crime.

I keep my head down. I refuse to talk to anyone about the video. I'm glad no one in my family sees it. I keep thinking about Addie. I want to ask her what she was doing out there. I want to find out what happened. But the way she looked at me when she was on those stairs, you would have thought was the one holding the knife and that I had just plunged it into her chest. I decide to wait and see what happens. Maybe the whole thing will blow over. She'll be back at school, some people will give her a hard time, and that will be that.

But that isn't that. Addie isn't at school on Monday. She isn't there Tuesday or Wednesday either. On Thursday, I get called down to the office. The cops are there. So are my parents.

"Sit down, Neely," Ms. LaPointe says. She's one of the vice-principals. "These officers want to ask you some questions."

I glance at my mom. She looks upset. My dad is stone-faced.

I sit.

The cops explain to me that the school computer has been hacked and that the school has asked them to look into it. They say they got help from a computer expert from the city and that he was able to trace the computer that was involved. It's mine.

"Did you hack into the school computer, Neely?" one of the cops asks.

"No."

"Neely, we know your computer was involved. Did you let someone else use it?"

I think of Kayla and Jen. I think of them sticking together and of Kayla's threat. I think about getting into trouble no matter what I say.

"I don't know anything about it."

"What about that video?" the cop asks. "You're in it. And the link for it was emailed to the whole school from your computer."

"I don't know anything about that either."

My dad clucks in disgust.

"Your mother tells me you've been running with a new crowd. Are they involved?"

Kayla will deny it. Jen and Shayna will back her up. They'll back each other up. And no one is recognizable. No one except me.

"The school is laying charges for hacking the computer, Neely," the cop says. "If there was some charge for what you did to that girl, I'd pursue that too."

"The school has a policy," Ms. LaPointe says. "What you did is cyber-bullying. There will be consequences."

The next thing I know, I'm arrested and taken to the police station. Class is still in, but that doesn't stop kids from looking out the window and seeing me. The news will be all over school in no time.

My dad calls a lawyer, who doesn't seem all that interested in hearing my side of the story. He just wants me to keep my mouth shut until he can get me released to my parents. Which he does. My dad takes me home. He doesn't say a single word the whole way there. He just drives and parks and lets me out of the truck. As I walk up to the house, he strides out to the barn as if he can't wait to put distance between us.

I go straight to my room, even though I hear my mother in the kitchen.

It isn't long before she's knocking at my door, asking if she can come in.

I tell her yes. Might as well. She's going to do it anyway.

She sits on the end of my bed. "Do you want to tell me what happened?"

"I made a mistake," I say. What I don't say is that Kayla planned this whole thing. She wasn't just out to get Addie—she was out to get me too. And she got me good.

"I can't believe you did what they say. Not all by yourself, anyway." My mom reaches out to touch my leg. I find myself recoiling. I hate myself for it. "Did those other girls have anything to do with it?"

She asks it as if it's a question, but the look on her face tells me she knows it for a fact.

"That girl Kayla," she says. "She was trying too hard to flatter me.

Maybe I'm wrong, but I got the impression she was making fun of me somehow."

I start to cry. I throw myself into my mother's arms. I love her so much.

Chapter Fourteen

I tell my mother everything. She advises me to tell the lawyer. The lawyer says, "It was your computer, and it's going to be your word against three girls who sound like they have their story pretty much together."

"Then the police will just have to talk to them," my mom says.

The lawyer doesn't answer. He asks me, "Those boys who were there— do you know who they were?"

I shake my head. "I didn't see their faces. It was too dark. And they were wearing masks."

"I see."

"Those girls know who they were," my mom says.

"And they're not telling," my dad says. He sounds angry, but I can't tell at who. I hope it's not me.

The lawyer's sharp eyes are still on me. "Did you actually see that girl, Jen, hack into the school computer?"

"No." I didn't pay the least attention to what Jen was doing. I was too focused on impressing Kayla.

The lawyer is silent for a moment. He caps his pen and slides his notepad back into his briefcase. "I'll talk to the school and see if they're willing to take Neely's record into consideration. Maybe they'll agree to drop the charges. I'll talk to the police, too, and see if they can make any headway with those girls. But I can't promise anything."

He makes no headway. Kayla's mother freaks out when the cops show up to question her daughter about something the police have already established was done by someone else. She contacts Jen's parents and gets Jen's mom all worked up, and the two of them get a lawyer. Shayna's parents contact Kayla's mom. Together they form a united front to protect their daughters against this slander from some local farm girl—me. All three girls are forbidden by their lawyers to talk to the police.

All three sets of parents, led by Kayla's mom, contact the school and demand that the school do something about these accusations against their daughters. They get their lawyers to make threats, too, if the harassment of their daughters continues while the local farm girl—they always refer to me as the farm girl—gets preferential treatment even though it's known beyond a shadow of a doubt what her role in all this has been. Kayla's mom also points out, in person, that her daughter has no reason to persecute any student for any reason—why would she?

For a day or two, it looks like the school is going to let me off with a suspension—at least, that's what the lawyer says. But then the school board gets involved. It seems that two of the school trustees, businessmen, have been contacted by Kayla's father, who has been enlisted to come to the defense of his darling daughter's reputation.

"They're pressing charges after all," the lawyer says. "They're going to allow you to go back to school, but you're not to have anything to do with any of those girls. You're also not allowed to use any of the computers at school."

"It could be worse," my mom says, squeezing my hand.

"Oh," says the lawyer, getting ready to stand up, "you're also forbidden to have any contact with Addie Murch. Her parents have taken out a restraining order."

"What?! But I didn't—"

I stop. Because, as far as anyone can see, I did. I look down at the table. Tears sting my eyes. I made a mistake. The least I can do now is take the punishment.

"Okay," I say.

Chapter Fifteen

It turns out I don't have to worry about the restraining order because Addie doesn't come back to school. There's a rumor going around that her parents are homeschooling her, but I never find out if it's true because I can never get up the nerve to ask anyone how she is doing, not after that first time when

I approach John, my whole body shaking, to ask if he's seen her around.

He looks down at me. His face is hard and mean.

"You think I'm going to say anything about her?" His voice is as hard as his face. "Why did you have to drag me into it?"

I feel my cheeks ignite like a bush-fire in a drought. Kids, caught by the sharpness of his voice, have turned to look. One of them is Kayla. She smirks at me. I slink away. Really, I wish I could run away and never come back.

Kids don't talk to me. They don't give me a hard time, but they don't go out of their way to talk to me either. It's as if they've decided, after they all had their big laugh at Addie's expense, that I am beneath contempt. At first I'm enraged. Who do they think they are? They were never her friends. They never cut her any slack. They never made any effort to get to know her.

And they laughed.

They all watched that video—no way they can tell me they didn't—and they talked about it with other kids. And they had a good laugh.

Now they're judging *me*?

I wait and wait for my case to be disposed of, as the lawyer likes to put it. It takes forever.

"Not like TV, is it?" the lawyer says, smiling for what is probably the first time ever.

Finally, weeks and weeks later, he tells me he's set up a meeting with the school board's lawyer and that if all goes well, I will probably get away with a suspended sentence. He adds that letting time go by means letting tempers cool—something he can say only because he hasn't been walking around at my school in my skin this whole time.

"By the way," he says, "all the court orders remain in effect until that time.

I don't want any surprises, okay, Neely? And trust me, neither do you."

The meeting is three days away when Addie walks into Mr. Grayson's class.

I feel everyone's eyes go to her and then to me.

I feel her eyes search me out.

I feel the heat rise in my cheeks. I want to look at her, but I can't make myself do it. It's been months. She took out a restraining order against me. She obviously thinks I'm the one who was behind what happened. She hates me.

Still, I want to talk to her. At least, that's what I tell myself. But no matter how many times I try to lift my eyes, I can't make myself do it. It's been too long. Too much water has gone under the bridge, as my grandpa would say. Addie thinks I did that horrible thing to her. She actually believes I'm behind it. She thinks I'm a monster.

What I really am, right at this moment, is a coward. When the bell rings, I flee, even though I know Kayla and Jen and Shayna will laugh at me for it. I tell myself that when it's all over, I'll go to Addie and tell her exactly what happened. I tell myself I'll do it even though I'm pretty sure she won't believe me. I have to set the record straight, don't I?

I'll swallow the shame and, yes, the anger I feel—how could she believe I would do such a thing?—and I'll tell her exactly what happened. She can choose whether or not she wants to believe me.

In the meantime, I flee. I go to my locker. I ignore the whispers I hear behind me. I know perfectly well who it is—Kayla and Jen and Shayna. I ignore the looks of the other kids too. I ignore them all.

And then I catch a glimpse of her—Addie—out of the corner of my eye. She's staring at me, and I know what she's thinking. I wish she'd come up to me, but she doesn't. Good old Addie, still chicken even after all of this. She watches me, thinking the worst of me, and there's nothing I can do, not today, except turn and walk away.

Next week, I tell myself. I'll talk to her next week.

Norah McClintock has written many bestselling novels, including *She Said/ She Saw, Back* and *Guilty*. Norah lives in Toronto, Ontario.

orca soundings

The following is an excerpt from
another exciting Orca Soundings novel,
Masked, by Norah McClintock.

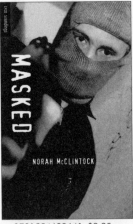

9781554693641 $9.95 PB
9781554693658 $16.95 LIB

WHEN DANIEL ENTERS A CONVENIENCE

store on a secret mission, he doesn't expect
to run into anyone he knows. That would ruin
everything. When Rosie shows up, she's hoping
to make a quick getaway with her waiting
boyfriend. But the next person through the door
is wearing a mask and holding a gun. Now
things are getting complicated.

Chapter One

Daniel

"Uh, do you have a bathroom I can use?" I'm ready with an excuse for when the man behind the counter says no. I thought long and hard to come up with it. You have to when you're asking to use the bathroom in a convenience store, which doesn't have to provide one the way restaurants do. I have to get yes for an answer if my mission is going to be a success.

The man behind the counter scowls. He peers at me from under gray eyebrows that look like steel wool. Is he on to me? Does he suspect?

"What about your coffee and taquito?" he says. "Are you still going to want those?"

"Yeah. And a two-liter cola and the latest *Wrestling World*, if you have it." I throw those in to improve my chances of getting a yes.

"We have it. What about *Wresting Today*? You want that too?" His piggy little eyes drill into me. I see immediately where he's going. If I want to use the facilities, I'm going to have to cough up some more money. I take another glance at the magazine rack.

"And *Wrestling Connoisseur*," I say. What the heck—I'm getting paid enough. A few magazines aren't going to make a dent in my paycheck.

"Through the door beside the coolers and down one flight," the man behind the counter says.

As I head down the narrow aisle toward the coolers, I glance in the security mirror at the back of the store. The man at the counter, the owner, is watching me.

Going through the door beside the big Coke-sponsored cooler is like stepping from Oz back into Kansas. The tile floor in the store sparkles. The wooden floor on the other side of the door is dingy, scuffed and slightly warped. The lights in the store are blindingly bright. On the other side of the door there is only a single naked lightbulb that makes the places it doesn't hit look inky and a little spooky. The walls of the store are chockablock with neatly displayed and colorful products. The walls of the small room are bare except for a car dealership calendar that hangs from a nail directly above a battered old table and chair. On the table is an adding machine—I didn't even know those still existed. Next to it is a two-drawer olive-green filing cabinet. On the wall, in an ancient fixture with a pull chain, is another naked lightbulb. This is where the store owner does his accounts. To the left of the door is a flight of wooden stairs. But I don't go down it.

Instead, I listen. It's quiet in here. It's also quiet out in the store. I tiptoe over to the desk. I'd been expecting a computer, but there isn't one. I open the top drawer of the filing cabinet. It's jammed with files. I thumb through them, looking for the one I've been sent to find. I don't see it. I close that drawer, open the next one and thumb through more folders.

Bingo! There it is, neatly labeled.

I pull it out and scan the sheets inside. They look like the ones that were described to me. I dig the miniature camera—a spy camera, if you can believe it—out of my pocket and photograph every sheet. I put everything back into the folder and replace the folder in the file cabinet. I tuck the camera into my pocket. I start back to the door.

Before I get there, I hear the man behind the counter yell something— a name. I'm about to push the door open and go back into the store when I hear a different voice—a familiar one. I decide to wait. If I go out there, I'll be recognized. If I'm recognized, I'll be exposed. If I'm exposed, I'll have to abort my mission. And if I abort... let's just say I don't want to kiss my paycheck goodbye.

orca soundings

For more information on all the books
in the Orca Soundings series, please visit
www.orcabook.com.